The Grey Lady and
the Strawberry Snatcher

by MOLLY BANG

Simon & Schuster Books for Young Readers

SIMON & SCHUSTER BOOKS FOR YOUNG READERS
An imprint of Simon & Schuster Children's Publishing Division
1230 Avenue of the Americas
New York, New York 10020
Copyright © 1980 by Molly Bang
All rights reserved including the right of reproduction
in whole or in part in any form.
Simon & Schuster Books for Young Readers is a trademark of Simon & Schuster
15 14 13 12 11 10
Printed in Hong Kong
Library of Congress Cataloging-in-Publication Data

Bang, Molly.
The grey lady and the strawberry snatcher.

Summary: The strawberry snatcher tries to wrest the
strawberries from the grey lady but as he follows her
through shops and woods he discovers some delicious
blackberries instead.
[1. Stories without words.   2. Strawberries—
Fiction] I. Title.
PZ7.B2217Gr 1986   [E]   85-29224
ISBN 0-02-708140-0

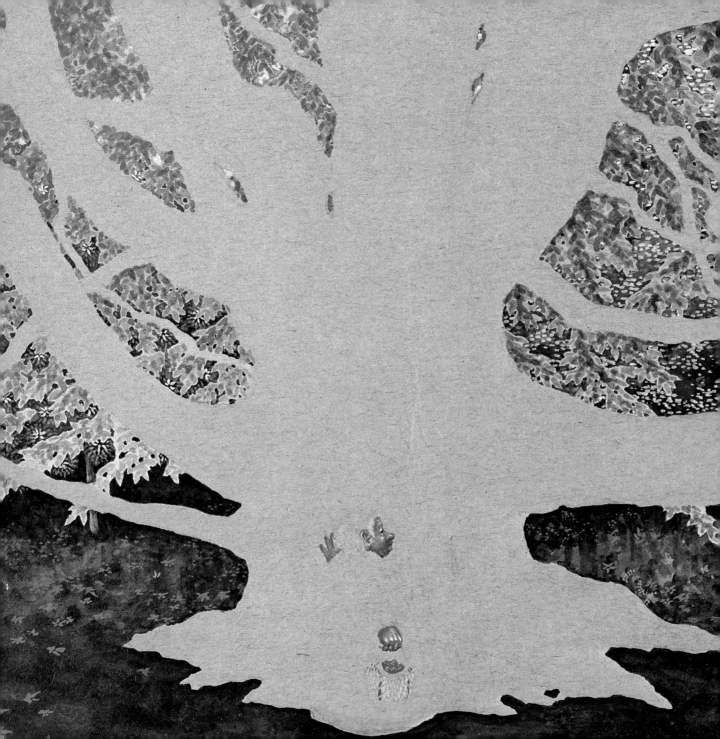

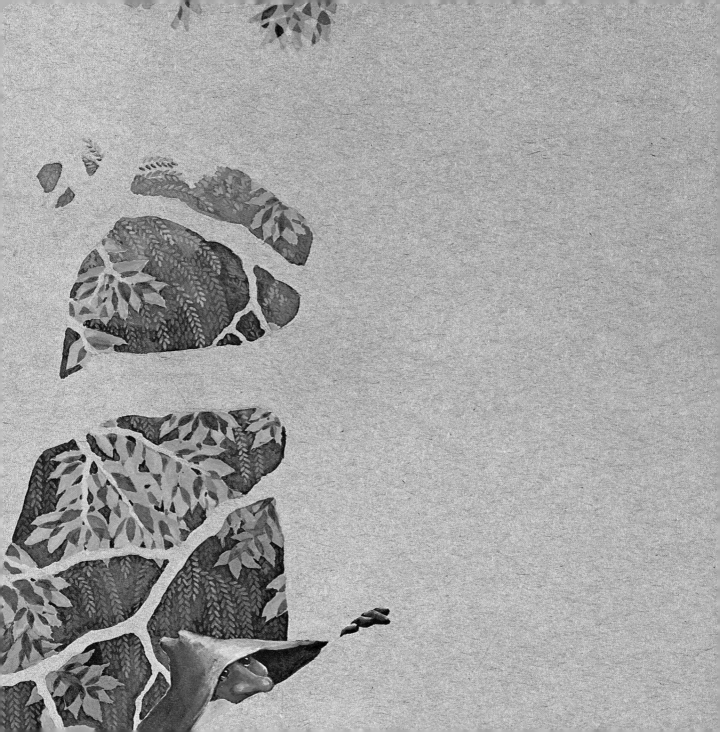

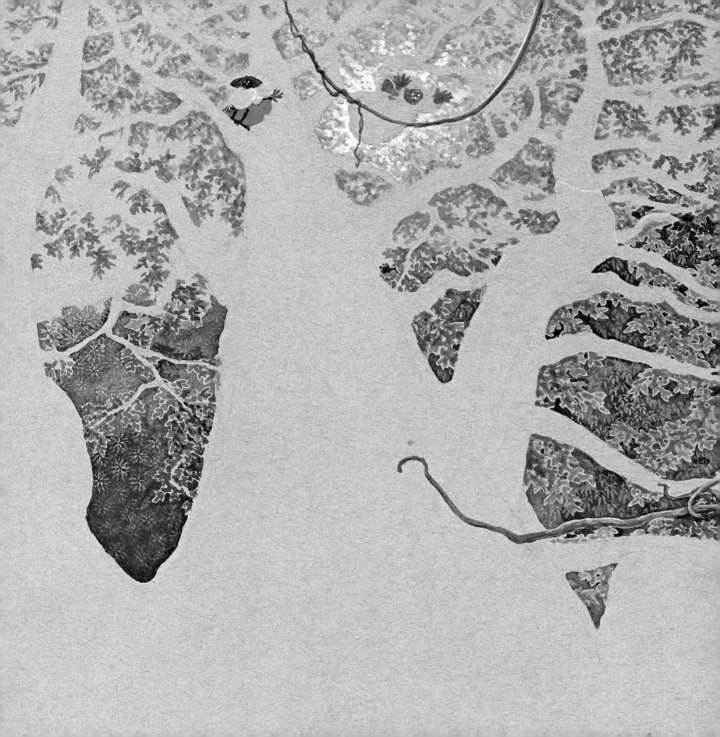